This edition published by Scholastic Inc., 557 Broadway, New York, NY 10012,
by arrangement with Little Tiger Press. SCHOLASTIC and associated logos
are trademarks and/or registered trademarks of Scholastic Inc.
Distributed by Scholastic Canada Ltd, Markham, Ontario
Original edition published in English by LITTLE TIGER PRESS,
an imprint of Magi Publications, London, England, 2009.

ISBN-10: 1-848-95014-4
ISBN-13: 978-1-84895-014-6
Printed in China
2 4 6 8 10 9 7 5 3 1

For Katie, with love ~ P B

For Laura, Grace and Oscar ~ L W

On a wild and windy day,
round about the end of May,
a great and gusting gale
blew the washing clean away.

Socks and vests, a woolly hat,
but far worse than all of that,
young Charlie's Superhero Underpants.

PO W!

As it soared into the sky,
the washing billowed, flapped, and swirled,
until it slowly scattered
to all corners of the world.

Though they searched for days and nights, with boats and planes and satellites, they found **no trace** of Charlie's Underpants.

They had POW!
across the front,
in giant letters,
bold and black,

POW!

woof

CITY
NEWS

SAVE
MONEY
012374

BUY
NOW

$50

Mom Please
wash Super
Pants...
Charlie x

Stop bar
Robbery!

UR
save

$2.50

Kerzap! Splat!
Oof!

with KERZAP! and OOF!
and SPLAT! a little smaller
on the back.

BOY
WONDER!
A

WINNER
BEST SUPER
HERO

And villains would take fright
as Charlie pulled his pants up tight.
His Scarlet Superhero
Underpants.

Charlie packed
some sandwiches,
some sardines,
and some soap,

a mirror, fan, and toothbrush,
and a big brass telescope.

"Don't worry and don't wait," he said.
"I may be back quite late.
But I've got to find my
Scarlet Underpants."

Charlie's Press Conference

PRESS
Chit
chat
mag

PRESS
Daily
Bugle

First, Charlie grabbed a ride
with a band in a balloon,
and they crossed the choppy Channel
to a bouncy, brassy tune.

Then, they saw
a fine French fox,
wearing sister Sophie's socks,
but no sign of Charlie's Underpants.

Angleterre

Culotte

Charlie hiked across
the endless plain of Serengeti,
where the insects made him itchy
and the sunshine made him sweaty.

There he saw a lion,
with a stripy shirt and tie on,
But no Scarlet Superhero Underpants.

Charlie climbed and clambered
up the plateau of Peru,
where the breeze that blows at night
makes you shiver through and through,

He found
a pair of llamas
wearing brother Ben's pajamas,

but he couldn't find his
Scarlet Underpants.

Charlie searched the length
of the mighty Mississippi,
though the Mississippi's muddy
and the mud's all soft and slippy.

And an alligator sat
wearing Grandpa's woolly hat,
but it wasn't wearing Charlie's Underpants.

Charlie was fed up.
He felt lonely, tired, and small,
on a steep and snowy hillside
in the mountains of Nepal.

When suddenly he saw
in that land of ice and cold,
a huge and hairy creature,
something wondrous to behold.

Charlie blinked and rubbed his eyes.
It couldn't be . . .

it could . . .

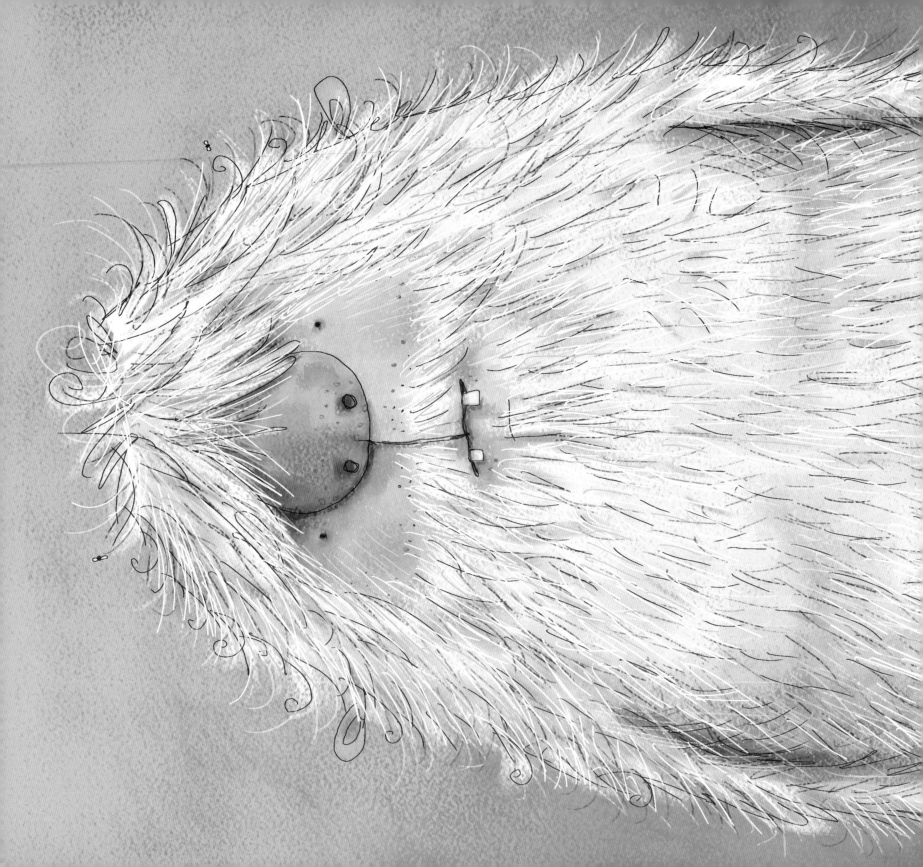

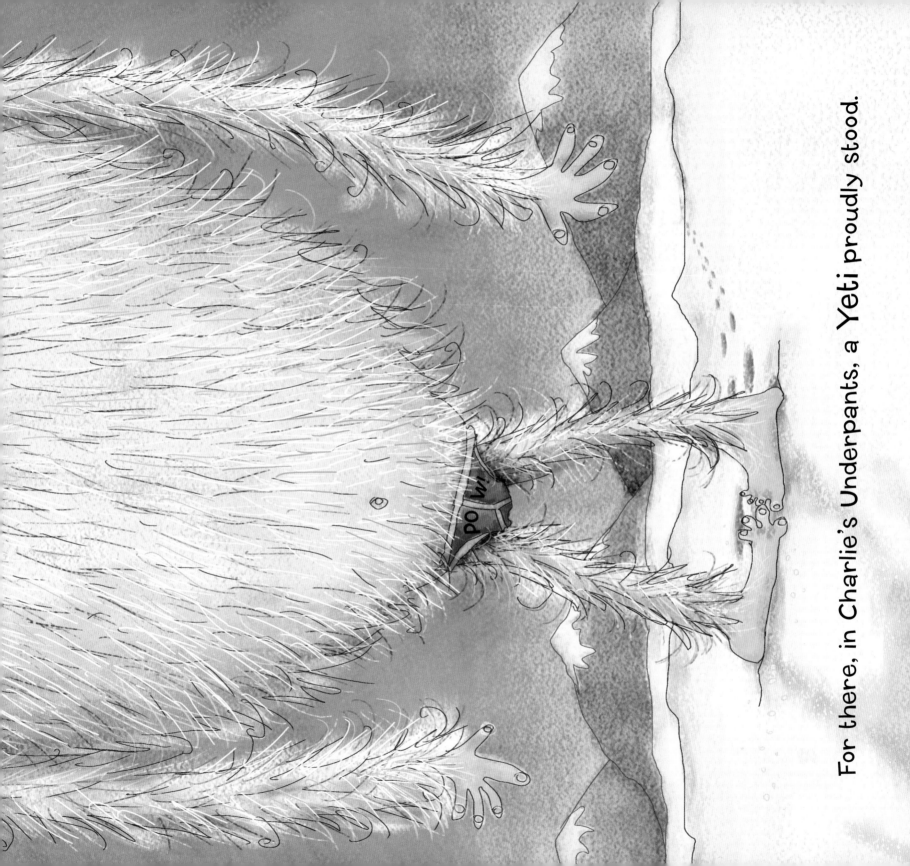

For there, in Charlie's Underpants, a Yeti proudly stood.

"My underpants!" cried Charlie. "They're the ones I love the most."

"But they're mine now," growled the Yeti, "and they keep me warm as toast!"

"I'll swap you," Charlie said.
"You'll be snug from toes to head,
if you'll give me back my Scarlet Underpants."

Charlie thanked the Yeti
and he pulled his pants up tight.
They had POW! across the front,
so he'd put them on just right.

He raised one arm up high, and he flew into the sky . . .

In his Scarlet Superhero

Underpants!